**EVERY
LITTLE THING
MATTERS**

Do you love nature like Lottie? Do you care
for every little thing on our planet?

Then you can help.
Every little thing YOU do matters A LOT!

Samira

Look out for this sticker for
tips on how YOU can help nature!

BY **JANE CLARKE** ILLUSTRATED BY **JAMES BROWN**

LOTTIE L♥VES NATURE

Frog Frenzy

FIVE QUILLS

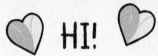 **HI!**

My name is Lottie and I love nature!

♡ LOTTIE ♡

← When I grow up,
I am going to be a
wildlife show presenter
like Samira Breeze
who presents
Every Little Thing.

EVERY
LITTLE THING
MATTERS

People are part of nature.
If nature thrives so do we!

I am keeping notes about lots
of cool stuff about nature,
wildlife and the Earth.

EVERY LITTLE THING MATTERS!

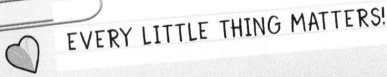

MY PETS

Did you know that a fully-grown macaw can weigh as much as a cat?

Did you know dogs are descended from wolves?

EINSTEIN

NACHO

NATURE NOTE

There are hundreds of different types of parrots, including budgerigars. Parrots love to mimic people, and imitate noises. They can live as long as humans.

I live with my mum and my twin brother Al. He hates spiders, but loves Science!

To the next generation of nature lovers in my family:
Angelina, Samantha, Elowyn and Pippa x – JC
For all the pupils at Nottingham Girls' High School, J.B.

LOTTIE LOVES NATURE: FROG FRENZY

First published in Great Britain in 2020 by Five Quills
93 Oakwood Court, London W14 8JZ

www.fivequills.co.uk

Five Quills and associated logos are a trademark of Five Quills Ltd.

Text copyright © Jane Clarke 2020
Illustrations copyright © Five Quills 2020

Edited by Natascha Biebow at Blue Elephant Storyshaping
Designed by Amy Cooper

A CIP record for this title is available from the British Library

ISBN 978 1 912923 07 6

1 3 5 7 9 10 8 6 4 2

Printed and bound in Great Britain by Clays Ltd, Elcograf S.p.A.

MIX
Paper from
responsible sources
FSC® C018072
www.fsc.org

CONTENTS

1   Parrots and Plans   1

2   Import-ant Ants   16

3   Sticky Stuff   31

4   Worm Squirm   54

5   Pond Life   69

6   Frog Frenzy   93

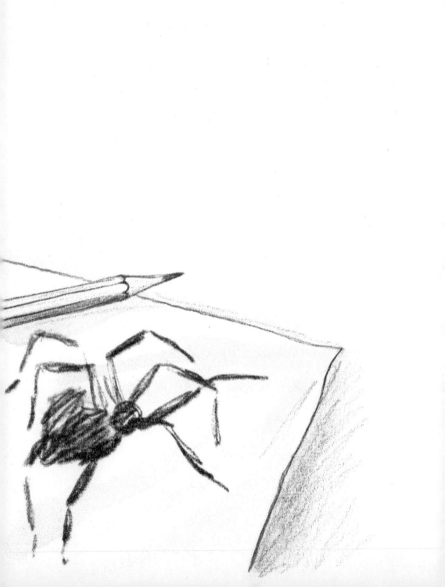

Parrots and Plans

Lottie Boffin lay on her tummy sketching an enormous spider. Her favourite wildlife show, 'Every Little Thing', was coming to an end. The presenter, Samira Breeze, smiled at the camera and announced, "Don't forget to send in your nature notes if you want to win a place on our annual wildlife adventure. The winners will have a chance to be a presenter, like me."

Fizzy bubbles of excitement whooshed through Lottie's body. She LOVED nature. It was her dream to win that prize!

"And remember," Sam continued, "you can help your local wildlife by creating a small pond in your garden from a recycled container, just like we showed you on this programme. Every little thing matters!"

"I can use the old dustbin lid to make a pond," Lottie thought. "That'll get frogs into the garden, AND make a great page in my nature notebook."

"I'll go and make one right now!" She jumped to her feet, startling her snoozing dog, Einstein.

WOOF! he barked in alarm.

There was a flapping of bright red, blue and gold feathers and an indignant **SQUUUUUAWK!**

Lottie giggled. Her parrot always made her laugh. She had inherited Nacho from Great Aunt Pru, who had re-homed him from a rescue centre.

From the instant he first met Lottie, Nacho had decided that she was his new human being.

Nacho folded his wings and opened his beak. **WOOF!**

Lottie groaned. Nacho did a very good imitation of Einstein, and he loved winding him up.

WOOF! WOOF! WOOF! Einstein retorted.

"It's a good thing the Goods are on holiday," Lottie murmured.

Their neighbours, the Goods, didn't like noise at all.

"Shhh!" Lottie told Einstein.

"**SHHH!**" Nacho muttered to himself as Lottie found a doggy chew and made Einstein sit quietly for it.

Now, who could she ask to help with the pond? Her best friend, Filip, had gone off to visit his relatives, and Mum was busy in the shop. Her twin brother Al had disappeared into the garage after breakfast to work on his top-secret science experiment, making a time machine. Lottie went to find him.

Al was staring at a heap of bike parts.

"Can you help me make a pond?" she asked.

"Sorry," said Al. "Mum says I have to put our bikes back together and I've got the parts all muddled up." He scratched his head. "This is going to take me all day. Try asking the Parfitts."

Mr Parfitt and his ten year-old son Noah had recently moved into the empty house next door.

"Mr Parfitt won't want to help me make a pond." Lottie shuddered at the thought of what Mr Parfitt had done to his garden. It used to have grass and lots of flowers and bushes like her own back garden. It had even had a pond – perfect for frogs and insects and all sorts of wildlife. But, as soon as they'd settled in, Mr Parfitt had turned it into a golf putting green, with six holes with flags in them.

"Mr Parfitt says he doesn't like nature, he likes golf." Lottie sighed.

"He likes things to be neat and tidy."

"What about Noah? He might help," Al suggested.

"I'll see if he's around." Lottie went outside and carefully stepped up on the rim of the big old flowerpot next to the fence. When she stood on that she could just about see over into next door's garden.

Mr Parfitt was jumping up and down on his fake grass. There was no sign of Noah.

Nacho copied Mr Parfitt and bobbed his head up and down too.

"Hola!" he squawked. Lottie knew that he'd lived with Great Aunt Pru in South America and had been rescued there as a fledgling, so it wasn't surprising that he still said hello to everyone in Spanish.

"Ah, Lottie!" Mr Parfitt greeted her with a wave of his golf club. "Please don't let your parrot fly over my garden again. He seems to think it's a good place for . . . um . . . er . . . his toilet needs. I have enough trouble with the ants today. They're all over the place. I'm afraid they'll get into the house just when Petunia is coming round for tea."

"Petunia!" screeched Nacho.

"Who's Petunia?" Lottie asked.

Mr Parfitt's face went red. "She's my new golfing partner," he said. "I can't wait for her to see my putting green."

"What if she likes gardens that have flowers in them?" Lottie asked.

"Oh, Petunia doesn't like plants."
Mr Parfitt snorted. "She says they
make a garden look untidy. She's a
very tidy person."

"Like you," Lottie commented,
gripping hold of the fence as the flowerpot she was standing on began to tilt.

"She is very like me!" Mr Parfitt said
in delight. "I want everything to be
perfect for her. Noah's been helping
me bake a cake for tea. But, before
she arrives, I need to work out what
to do about these ants. I think there's
a nest . . . " He crouched down and
stared at them.

Lottie jumped off the flowerpot just in time to stop it from tipping over. There was a startled **SQUAWK!** as Nacho took off from her shoulder and circled over the Parfitts' garden.

Lottie quickly stepped back up on the flowerpot.

"Nacho!" she called. He flew down to her shoulder and nibbled her ear affectionately.

But it was too late.

One of the flags on Mr Parfitt's golf course was spattered in parrot poop.

Import-ant Ants

Lottie checked anxiously to see if Mr Parfitt had noticed. He was still staring down at the ants.

"Phew!" Lottie breathed a sigh of relief. With any luck, she could clean off the poop before he saw it. "Where's Noah?" she asked.

"Hmmm?" said Mr Parfitt distractedly. "Yes, it's as I suspected," he sighed as

he stood up. "There is a nest. Ants are such a nuisance! What's the point of them anyway?"

"Samira Breeze says every little thing is important," Lottie said, "And that includes ants."

"Who on earth is Samira Breeze?" Mr Parfitt sounded puzzled.

"She presents 'Every Little Thing'," Lottie explained. "You know, the show I watch. Every year, it runs a competition, and the winners of the best nature notes get a chance to be wildlife presenters with Sam Breeze in amazing places like Alaska and Africa!

I'm going to try to win it this year!"

"That's all very well," Mr Parfitt said, "but that doesn't explain why ants are important."

"Without ants, anteaters would be extinct!" Lottie told him. "And Sam says ants are important for plants because they eat the aphids that eat plants. Plus all sorts of birds and animals eat ants. They're a very important source of food for wildlife." Lottie made a mental note to include that information in her nature notes later.

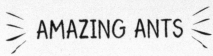

AMAZING ANTS

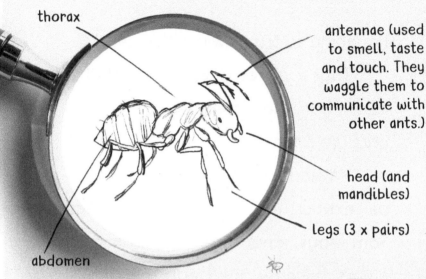

thorax

antennae (used to smell, taste and touch. They waggle them to communicate with other ants.)

head (and mandibles)

legs (3 x pairs)

abdomen

Samira says ANTS are important.

Ants dig tunnels and turn up the earth to keep the soil healthy.

Good for growing plants and crops for our food!

Ants eat plants, insects and even dead animals.

Many amphibians, birds and insects think ants are yummy too.

MY MINI-EXPERIMENT:

I tried leaving out crisps and cake. More ants came to the cake!

Ants like sugary things best.

A single ant can carry up to 50 times its own bodyweight. Ants often work together to move bigger objects – like cake ☺.

EVERY LITTLE THING MATTERS

I made a home for ants in my garden under a pile of rocks.

ROCKS

"Well, I don't like ants," Mr Parfitt grumbled. "My grandmother always poured boiling water on ants' nests to kill them. I'll go and put the kettle on!"

Lottie shuddered. "Please don't do that!" she begged. "Let me get some sugar to make a trail for them to follow over the fence. They're welcome in my garden."

"Very well," Mr Parfitt said. "Just as long as it's only a tiny bit of sugar. I don't want my nice new turf turning into a sticky mess just when Petunia's coming over for the first time. That reminds me. I need to put the finishing touches to the cake that Noah helped me bake for her."

He turned and headed towards the back door. Just then, it opened and Noah sloped into the garden.

"Hola!" squawked Nacho.

"Hi," grunted Noah.

"Can you help me dig a pond in my garden?" Lottie asked him.

Noah peered at Lottie from behind the hair that flopped over his eyes. "I might as well," he said. "I have to keep fit if I want to be chosen to be one of the first people to live on Mars."

"That's not going to happen any time soon, is it?" Lottie said.

"It won't be that long," Noah said seriously. "Space engineers and inventors are busy preparing to send the first spaceship there soon!"

"I'm never going to Mars. I'm staying on Earth and helping to save all the wonderful wildlife and plants here," Lottie told him. "If we don't do something to help them now, our planet will have even more problems in the future."

"But the future's exciting!" Noah said, brushing an ant off his leg.

"Engineers and computer scientists like me are developing new technologies all the time . . ."

"Like what?" Lottie stared at Noah's shoes. He might be clever, but he'd forgotten to tie his laces.

Noah thought for a moment. "These ants," he said. "They're like little robots."

"Robots?" Lottie sounded puzzled.

"Yes. Computer scientists studied ants' behaviour and invented robots called swarm robots."

"What for?"

"Swarm robots communicate with each other, like ants," Noah explained. "They can do important jobs like looking for missing people when there is a disaster, and performing tricky surgeries. In the future we'll probably all be using robotics so cars will drive themselves—"

"All that takes a lot of energy," Lottie interrupted. "Using too much fuel is why there's a climate emergency on Earth."

"Scientists are developing renewable energy sources all the time too," Noah pointed out.

"But it's taking too long!" Lottie said. "Nature is in danger and we need to do something now — even if it's only a little thing. Samira says every little thing matters. That's why I'm saving these ants."

"I thought you just wanted me to help you make a pond?" Noah sighed.

"I do," Lottie said. "That's one of the most important things I can do to help wildlife in my garden.

But first, stay where you are, I have to bring some sugar round to your house — or your dad will kill these ants . . ."

NOAH'S NEXT LEVEL: Robot Helpers

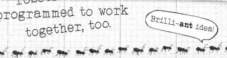

Sticky stuff

Lottie dribbled sugar out of the bag to create a thin trail that stretched from the ants' nest up to the fence.

"Can you get me a mug of water?" she asked Noah. "I have to make this line of sugar go up and over the fence, and the sugar needs something to stick to."

"If you're sure that's a good idea . . ."

"It is, but maybe you should tie your shoelaces so you don't trip up?" Lottie advised.

Noah grunted. He went into his house and reappeared with some water. His shoelaces were still undone.

Lottie held the mug above the fence and tipped the water so it dribbled down on both sides. Then she carefully sprinkled sugar onto the damp line she'd created.

Lottie stood back to admire her handiwork. The first ants had already discovered the sugar trail and were following it. Mr Parfitt would be pleased. Something thumped against her legs, interrupting her thoughts. Einstein had followed her into the Parfitts' garden.

His tail was wagging hard as he licked up the sugar trail.

"Don't do that!" Lottie ordered, grabbing him by the collar. Einstein gave her a big sticky sugary lick.

Slurp!

"Stop that," Lottie giggled. "You'll make Nacho jealous."

There was a loud *squawk!* Nacho threw his wings open and lunged at Einstein, knocking the bag of sugar out of Lottie's hand.

It flew into the air.

"Uh-oh!" Lottie gasped as a shower of sugar rained down on them.

Noah shook sugar off his head. "Dad will be cross when he sees this mess," he sighed.

"Don't just stand there. Help me clean it up!" Lottie frantically scooped as much sugar as she could back into the bag, but it was no good. Loads of sticky white granules were caught between the stiff fibres of the artificial grass. Noah and Lottie brushed at the sugar with their hands until it was spread out.

"You can't really see it now," Lottie said hopefully.

Nacho crunched across the sugary surface and poked his beak into the open back door, then strutted into the Parfitts' kitchen.

"Don't go in there!" Lottie shouted. She frantically tapped her shoulder. "Nacho, come here!"

Nacho fluttered obediently back onto Lottie's shoulder.

She scratched the downy feathers on his head. "Good boy!" she said, relieved. She didn't want to think what Mr Parfitt would say if Nacho made a mess in his pristine kitchen.

"Now the ants are sorted out, we can finally make our pond," Lottie said. She gestured for Einstein and Noah to follow her and headed to the Boffins' garage, where Al was hard at work.

Lottie knew she'd seen the old dustbin lid somewhere. Nacho stalked around the dusty garage floor as she looked for it.

"How are your time machine experiments going?" Noah asked Al as Lottie searched. The twins had let him into their secret.

"Slowly," groaned Al, holding up hands covered in dirty black oil. "Mum won't let me experiment with these bike gears."

"Where are you planning to time travel first?" Noah asked.

"I'm taking Mum back to see Dad," Al said matter- of-factly. "He died ages ago, but she still misses him a lot. After that, we can go anytime anywhere. Where would you choose to go?"

"To see the colony on Mars a hundred years from now," Noah told him. "That would be cosmic!"

"Awesome," Al agreed.

"Found it!" Lottie dragged out the old dustbin lid from behind a pile of paint tins and cardboard boxes.

"Found it!" Nacho echoed. He swooped out of the garage and perched on the fence to watch. Lottie gave Noah the lid to carry, while she carried a couple of spades into the garden. Einstein followed her out.

"Why use this old thing?" Noah asked. "You could get a brand new

NOAH'S NEXT LEVEL: Life On Mars?

No known life forms live on Mars. It is too cold and dusty to support life.

Mars is bombarded by solar and cosmic radiation dangerous to life as we know it.

Billions of years ago there was water on Mars. It is ice now!

What about unknown life forms?

Unmanned rockets landed robots on Mars. They map it, measure the climate, and drill for soil samples.

In the future, we plan to send manned missions to Mars.

See this red dust? That's why we call Mars the red planet.

What do you call a peanut in a spacesuit? **An astronut.**

Where can the astronauts park a space ship? **At a parking meteor.**

Human colonists like me will need to live inside domes. I'll need to wear a spacesuit outside.

plastic pond liner."

"Sam says it's important to recycle," Lottie explained. "Plastic pollutes the oceans and kills wildlife."

"That's not good," Noah agreed. "But sometimes plastic can be a very good thing."

"Can it?" Lottie sounded surprised.

"Engineers are replacing metals with plastics on aeroplanes and spacecraft to make them lighter, so they will use less fuel," Noah explained.

"That will be good for the Earth," Lottie agreed.

"And 3D printers can make just about anything out of plastic. Like prosthetic limbs that are made the exact size and shape for the person who needs one. We'll need 3D printers on Mars and plastic will be precious."

"So you'll reuse and recycle everything on Mars, just like we should

Help nature by cutting
down on plastics.
Reduce.
Reuse.
Recycle!

EVERY
LITTLE THING
MATTERS

be doing on Earth?"

"Yep," Noah said. "We'll have to. We can't take everything with us." Noah put down the lid under the old apple tree at the back of the garden.

Lottie looked up. "Sam said not to make a pond under trees," she said thoughtfully. "Too many leaves would fall in and clog it up . . ."

NOAH'S NEXT LEVEL:
Useful Plastics

Plastics are used in mobile phones, TVs, and computers.

Plastics help make lightweight afety gear, like bike helmets and child car seats.

Plastic can be recycled many times.

Properly used, plastic is fantastic! Don't be careless with it. Reduce, reuse, recycle!

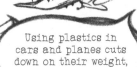

Using plastics in cars and planes cuts down on their weight, which saves fuel.

I like plastic when it's like my jokes – recycled.

Plastics are very important in medicine (for example syringes, tubes and knee implant parts).

"Let's put it somewhere where it will be partly in the shade and partly in the sun. I'm going to sow wildflowers here for the butterflies, but I haven't got round to it yet."

She handed Noah a spade. "You told me you need to keep fit. And by the way, your shoelaces are still undone."

"On Mars," Noah commented, "we will wear boots that don't need shoelaces and we'll have robots to dig out ponds."

"But you'll have to live in domes and you won't have any ponds!" Lottie retorted.

"We could have indoor ponds if we melt the ice," Noah said. "Living on Mars will be cosmic!"

"But it's a dead planet, not like Earth." Lottie marked out the area to dig with the edge of her spade. "I'd hate to live in a world without wildlife."

Nacho watched from the fence as Lottie marked out the area to dig with her spade.

Einstein gave a deep sigh and lay down with his head on his paws. Above him, Nacho stuck his head under his wing.

"They're taking a nap while we do all the work!" Noah laughed.

WILDLIFE MATTERS

Samira says we need to help wildlife because
every little thing (including us) depends on one another.
Everything we need can be found right here on Earth!

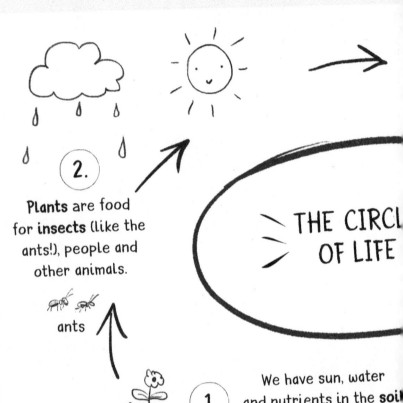

2.

Plants are food
for **insects** (like the
ants!), people and
other animals.

ants

> THE CIRCL
> OF LIFE

1. We have sun, water
and nutrients in the **soi**
so **plants** can grow.

Creatures big and small and plants all need each other!

EVERY LITTLE THING MATTERS

3. **Frogs** and **other creatures** eat the **insects**.

4. Birds and bigger creatures eat smaller creatures – like **frogs!**

5. When **creatures** die, worms and fungi break them down into nutrients in the **soil**.

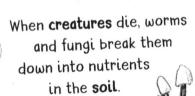

Worm Squirm

Lottie dug out a big spadeful of crumbly dirt. "Oh look!" she exclaimed, "I found an ammonite!"

Nacho gazed down curiously from his perch on the fence as she held out the fossil for Noah to see.

"That must be millions of years old!" Noah sounded impressed. "People find so many fossils on Earth," he said wistfully. "I hope we find some on Mars."

"Did anything ever live on Mars?" Lottie asked him. She popped the ammonite into her pocket so she could make a sketch of it later.

EXTINCTION

Our garden was once in a shallow sea!

Ammonites are fossils of extinct sea creatures. They died out 65 million years ago, along with most dinosaurs. Scientists think a huge asteroid hit Earth and they couldn't adapt to the new climate.

Nacho's distant relative!

Not all life on Earth at that time died out, though. Some dinosaurs evolved into birds.

"Maybe," Noah said hopefully, stamping his foot down on his spade. "Astrobiologists are looking, they just haven't found any signs of life yet."

"There are plenty of signs of life here." Lottie gently picked a worm out of the shovelful of dirt that Noah had discarded. It wriggled between her fingers as she went to fetch an old bucket that was lying on the grass. Al had used it for his water experiments so the handle was still a bit wobbly from when he'd whirled it round on a rope.

"Put any worms you find in here," she told Noah. "We have to be careful

not to hurt them. Sam says worms are very important because they improve the soil so more things grow in it."

Lottie paused for a moment as she stared at the worm wriggling round the bottom of the bucket. It was hard to tell which end was which, but she remembered Sam saying the head was closest to the thickest part. "Is there even soil on Mars?" she asked Noah.

"Yes, it's red and dusty," Noah said, using the tips of his fingers to pick up a big worm. He dropped it as it squirmed. "Ugh!" he shuddered.

"You're not scared of going to Mars, but you're scared of a worm?" Lottie giggled.

"I'm not scared!" Noah grabbed the

worm and held it at arm's length. He dropped it in the bucket.

"Better get used to it. You'll need worms on Mars if you ever want to grow things in the soil there." Lottie laughed. She carefully placed a handful of small soil-sprinkled worms into the bucket. She peered inside. There were eleven worms in total. The biggest was twice the length of her longest finger!

"Oh, we won't have to grow things in soil," Noah said dismissively. "At least not at first, while we're living in domes. We'll just add nutrients to water and grow our plants in that. It's called hydroponics."

He helped Lottie lay the dustbin lid on top of the hole they'd dug. It wasn't quite deep enough in the middle.

"You dig some more. I'll scout for worms," Lottie told Noah. She picked up the bucket.

"In the future we might use hydroponics to save space on Earth by growing things in towers instead of fields," Noah went on. "That way you can grow more things for people to eat," he explained.

NOAH'S NEXT LEVEL: Hydroponics

> Mostly, our food grows in the soil in fields. But we can also grow plants in water! This is called hydroponics.

On The Farm

In the fields, the sun, rain and nutrient-rich **soil** helps crops to grow big and strong.

> Lettuce be friends.

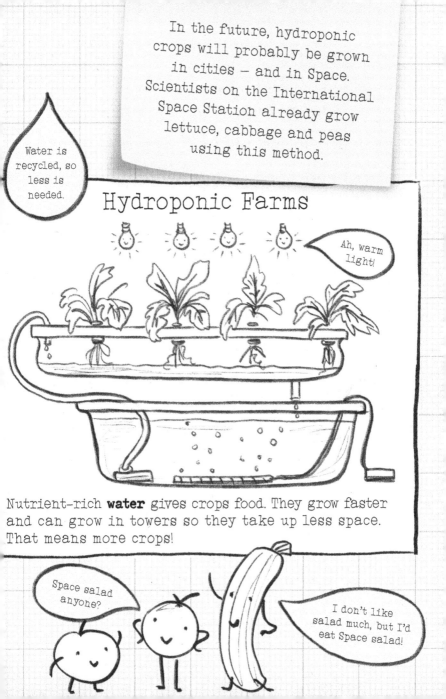

In the future, hydroponic crops will probably be grown in cities — and in Space. Scientists on the International Space Station already grow lettuce, cabbage and peas using this method.

Water is recycled, so less is needed.

Hydroponic Farms

Ah, warm light!

Nutrient-rich **water** gives crops food. They grow faster and can grow in towers so they take up less space. That means more crops!

Space salad anyone?

I don't like salad much, but I'd eat Space salad!

"Yooo hooo! Noah, Lottie, can you help me please?" The back gate banged open. Lottie stood up as Mr Parfitt strode purposefully towards them. He was wearing neatly-pressed yellow and green chequered trousers and a bright orange polo shirt.

Noah groaned. "I've never seen *that* outfit before," he said in a low voice. "Dad must've bought it to impress Petunia. I know he's been lonely since Mum left, and it's great that he's made a new friend, but I really hope he's not thinking about marrying her!"

Nacho took to the air and circled

just above Mr Parfitt's golfing cap, clicking his beak together.

"Nacho must think your dad's another parrot," Lottie whispered to Noah.

"Get that bird away from me!" Mr Parfitt yelled. He was so busy looking up, he didn't notice the hole they'd dug out for the pond.

BUMP! he tripped and landed on his bottom in the soft dirt and lay there, flailing his arms and legs.

Both Noah and Lottie automatically stretched out their hands to help him up. But Lottie had forgotten she was holding a bucket full of worms! A clump of them tipped out and landed in Mr Parfitt's lap, sprinkling him with soil.

"*Urgh!*" he yelled.

Awwwk! Nacho squawked.

The parrot fluttered down to perch on Mr Parfitt's golfing cap. He bobbed his head up and down excitedly and turned round so his tail feathers fell over Mr Parfitt's eyes.

Woof! Woof! Woof! Einstein barked.

Lottie and Noah glanced at one another, grinning madly. Luckily, Noah's dad couldn't see them trying not to laugh.

Pond Life

Lottie settled Nacho and Einstein back down to their naps, while Noah brushed soil off his Dad's back. Mr Parfitt's new golfing clothes didn't look so crisp and clean any more.

"What happened to the worms?" Lottie asked worriedly. "Are they okay?"

WONDERFUL WORMS

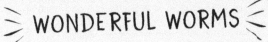

EVERY
LITTLE THING
MATTERS

Worms are nature's free fertilisers.
Worms break down leaves and grass and dead
things in the soil into nutrients that plants can use.
They eat and poop soil so that more
air and water gets into it.
They can eat their own weight in a day!

Juicy worms are
food for many
animals and birds.

I found lots of worms in my garden,
especially after it had rained.

They like to live under rocks, logs and near water.
They will love being close to my pond!

On rainy days worms come to the top of the soil.

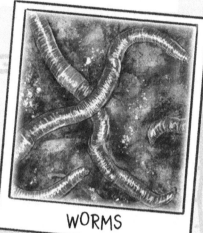

WORMS

≥ WORM FACTS: ≤

Worms have been around
since before the dinosaurs!
They are invertebrates.
There are over 2,000
different types of
earthworm.

No backbone.

No eyes.

Skin that 'breathes'.

No teeth.

No lungs.

No ears.

"Don't worry," Noah told her. "I put the worms back in the bucket." He turned to his dad. "I've brushed all the dirt off," he reassured him. "Petunia won't notice a thing!"

Mr Parfitt straightened his golf cap. "Thanks, Noah. Now, before I fell over, I was about to ask you two to

remove a frog from my golf course. It's hopping all over the place. Petunia doesn't like frogs. She says they are nasty, slimy creatures."

"Frogs aren't nasty!" Lottie exclaimed. "They're fascinating. I'll come and save it."

"Thank you! I don't have the time to mess around with a frog before Petunia arrives," muttered Mr Parfitt. "I still have to polish my golf shoes and finish icing her cake and Noah, you need to put on a clean T-shirt. She'll be here in five minutes, so you'll need to hurry!" He rushed off.

"The frog in your garden must be looking for its old pond," Lottie commented to Noah thoughtfully. "In the Spring, frogs make their way back to the pond they grew up in to find a mate and lay their eggs."

Noah groaned. "And Dad filled in the old pond so he could build his golf course, so the frogs will need a new pond."

"Exactly," agreed Lottie. "We need to finish our pond!"

She and Noah settled the old dustbin lid into the hole they had dug for it. It fitted perfectly now. Lottie piled up a small heap of rocks at one side. "So any wildlife that goes in can get out," she explained. She stood back to admire it. "It's looking good, isn't it?"

"It would be better with some water," Noah said.

"And pond weed and water plants to make the frog feel at home. I can use my pocket money to buy them from the garden centre later . . ."

Lottie thought for a moment. "Oh, no! I just remembered something!" She groaned. "We can't fill the pond with tap water and put the frog straight in it."

"Why not?" asked Noah.

"Because it has chlorine in it to make it safe to drink – and chlorine is dangerous for frogs and fish. Sam said tap water has to be left to stand for 48

hours to let the chlorine evaporate."
Lottie sighed. "What we need right
now is some rainwater."

"We have a rainwater barrel near
our back door," said Noah.

"Perfect!" Lottie exclaimed. She
carefully emptied the worms onto a
patch of soil and then handed Noah the
bucket. "You can fill up the pond, while I
catch the frog." Lottie glanced at Nacho
and Einstein. They both seemed to be
peacefully snoozing, but they each had
one eye open. "Don't
follow us next door!"
she ordered.

FROG LIFE CYCLE

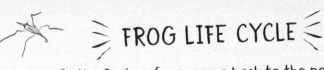

In the Spring, frogs come back to the pond where they were born so they can mate. (That's why they came back to Mr Parfitt's garden.)

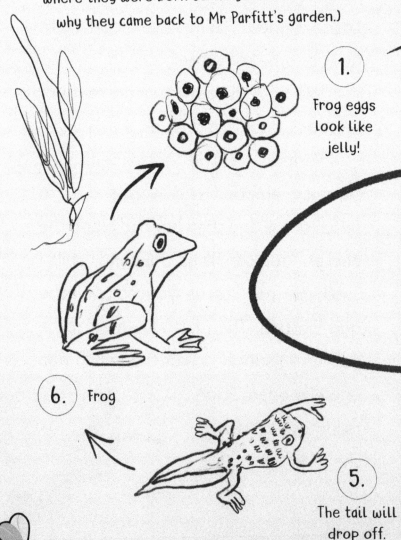

1.

Frog eggs look like jelly!

6. Frog

5.

The tail will drop off.

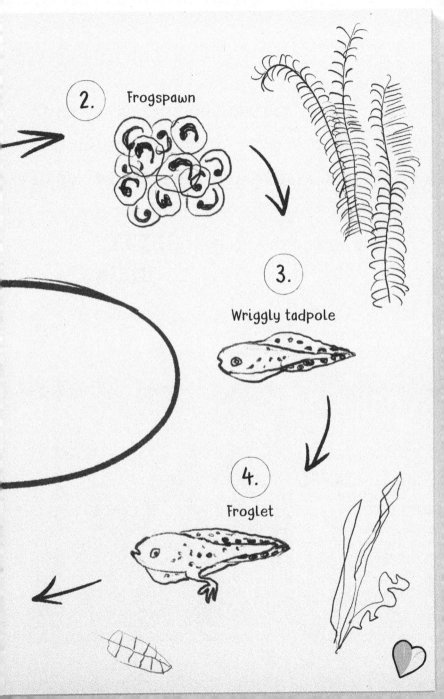

2. Frogspawn

3. Wriggly tadpole

4. Froglet

The frog was hopping all around the fake grass golfing green. Lottie stood as still as possible so she wouldn't frighten it. She was just about to coax it into her hand when **CLINK, CLUNK!**

Noah shuffled by, rattling the bucket handle on one of his trips to fill the pond. Startled, the frog hopped off again.

"**Shhhh! Tiptoe!**" Lottie said. She crouched down and waited.

At last, the frog sat still on the green, gently gulping to itself.

Lottie silently dropped to her hands and knees and crawled towards it. She held her breath and stretched out her arms.

"Got you!" Lottie held the frog gently, but firmly. Its head poked out of her cupped hands. It felt cool and smooth to her touch. It was amazing to think that it could breathe and absorb water through its skin.

"Is the pond full yet?" Lottie asked Noah when he reappeared.

"This is the last bucketful," Noah

told her as he refilled it from the rainwater barrel. "Just as well. This handle feels really wobbly." The bucket swung wildly as he picked it up.

"**Watch out!**" yelled Lottie at the top of her voice.

But her warning came too late. There was a **POP** and the bucket handle flew off.

"Hola!" squawked Nacho as water splashed everywhere.

Woof! Einstein added.

"I told them not to follow us!" Lottie groaned, cradling the startled frog in her hands.

SPLOSH!

Rainwater sloshed all over the ground and began to puddle near the Parfitts' back door.

"Maybe it will wash away the last of the sugar," Lottie said hopefully.

"Maybe," Noah shrugged.

Lottie watched him fill up the handle-less bucket from the Parfitts' water barrel and stagger off with it clutched to his chest to add it to the pond.

"Come on!" she told Nacho and Einstein. "Let's get this little frog into its new home in our garden."

Lottie knelt down beside the pond and gently opened her hands. The frog leapt into the water and quickly climbed out onto a rock.

"I think it likes our pond," she told Noah. "But I'm a bit worried it might be lonely. He, or she, needs some froggy friends."

Frogs push their eyeballs down into

their mouth to help them swallow.

Frogs breathe through their skin as well as their lungs.

Every different species of frog makes a different sound.
Some can be heard over a mile away!

The Javan flying frog
glides from tree to
tree by spreading
out the webs of skin
between its toes.

 The brightly-coloured South American
poison dart frog has toxic skin. One tiny
frog could kill more than ten humans!

Rooh-rooh!

Ribbit!

Croooak!

Peee-eee-p!

WARNING: amphibians can carry
salmonella germs on their skin,
so if you handle one, wash
your hands afterwards
with anti-bacterial soap.

Suddenly, a loud shriek came from the Parfitts' house. Al burst out of the garage. "What's happening?" he asked.

"No idea!" Lottie looked at Noah in alarm. Nacho flapped up into the air as they all raced next door to find out what was going on.

Frog Frenzy

Mr Parfitt was standing in his back doorway, looking distraught.

"Ants!" he shrieked. "Ants are all over the icing on Petunia's cake!" He took off his golf cap and ran his fingers through his hair. "I did so want everything to be perfect for her."

"It's okay, Dad," Noah said soothingly. "A few ants are not the end of the world."

"A few ants? There are hundreds of them!" Mr Parfitt glared crossly at Lottie. "This is your fault," he told her. "You said you'd lure the ants away to live in your garden!"

"Sorry!" Lottie apologised. "I'll help if you let me come in." She carefully stepped over the puddle by the back door. It was soaking away, but she suspected the water might be very sugary. She followed Mr Parfitt into his kitchen.

Mr Parfitt slumped down on a chair at the kitchen table and put his head in his hands. Ants were crawling all over

Petunia's cake. The ant trail started at the kitchen door. That's where Nacho had strutted in with his sugary footprints earlier, Lottie remembered with a pang of guilt. The ants tracked across the kitchen floor, and up the table leg.

"Don't worry," she said. "The ants haven't eaten much cake. I'll brush them off and Petunia will never know!"

"Ooh, do you really think you can save it?" Mr Parfitt sounded hopeful. He stood up and watched as Lottie quickly washed her froggy hands

in the sink, picked up the cake
and took it outside. She pulled
the door closed behind her.

Ribbet!

A frog hopped over Lottie's feet . . . and another, and another. Mr Parfitt's golf course was covered in leaping, croaking frogs! Noah and Al stared at them open-mouthed.

"I've never seen so many frogs before!" Noah gasped.

"They must have heard the first frog and come looking for a pond!" Lottie grinned. "We made a new one just in time. Isn't that great?"

"Shhh!" Noah hissed. "Maybe you can get them into the pond before Dad notices. I'll guard the door."

"Too late!" Lottie sighed. Mr Parfitt was already pushing it open.

"What's going on?" he asked suspiciously, taking a step outside.

The children watched in horror as Mr Parfitt's foot slipped on the damp patch of rainwater and sugar, and knocked the cake out of Lottie's hand.

It somersaulted into the air and landed **SPLAT**! on Mr Parfitt's head.

"Petunia's cake!" cried Mr Parfitt. Almost immediately he began to clutch his neck. "Ants! Ants!" he yelped, tearing off his shirt and golfing trousers. His underpants had pictures of little aliens on them.

"I bought him Martian underpants for Father's Day," Noah told Lottie and Al.

They giggled.

"I'm all sticky!" Mr Parfitt screamed, hopping up and down. "The ants are biting me!"

The Parfitts' back gate creaked open.

"Hello?" Petunia walked in, looking spotless in colourful golfing clothes.

"Hola!" called Nacho from high above her.

Petunia's eyes widened at the sight of Mr Parfitt and his Martian underpants.

Ribbit! Ribbit! A frog hopped onto her shiny golf shoe and sat there, gulping to itself.

The colour drained from Petunia's face. She seemed to be frozen to the spot. "**Argh! Get it off, get it off, get it off!!!!**" she shrieked.

"Pity the Mars spaceship isn't ready to go yet," Noah murmured. "We could escape to outer Space!"

"But I don't want to live on Mars," Lottie reminded him.

"Get it off! Get it off!

Get it off!" Nacho squawked as he flew round the garden, imitating Petunia to perfection.

Arooo! howled Einstein, excitedly.

SPLAT! Nacho pooped on another flag.

"You'd better escape home," Noah advised. He raised his voice above the noise. "I'll get Dad and Petunia inside."

Al grabbed Einstein's collar and dragged him away.

Lottie looked round at the chaos.

"All I wanted was to do a little thing to try to help the local wildlife," she sighed.

"Maybe it's easier to give up trying?" Noah suggested.

"Never!" Lottie said. "I'll come back and clean up the parrot poop and collect all the frogs when things have calmed down a bit. Right now, I have to write up my nature notes so I can win a place on Sam Breeze's next Wildlife Adventure."

"You've got a wildlife adventure going on here," Noah pointed out.

"You're right," Lottie said as she took Nacho back to her garden. "It's wild around here!"

Lottie couldn't help smiling. Every little thing in her garden was going to love the new pond, AND it would make a great page in her nature notebook.

☰ MY MINI POND ☰

Old lid (You can also use any container that holds water, like an old washing-up bowl.)

Slope of logs and rocks so that creatures can climb in and out safely.

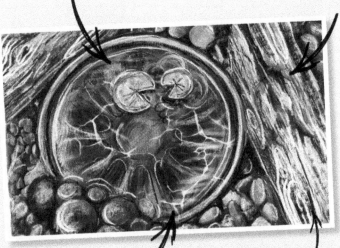

We dug out a hole to fit the lid.

A log or rocks and pebbles.

Sunny spot away from falling tree leaves.

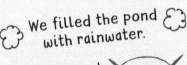
We filled the pond with rainwater.

Chlorinated tap water is bad for wildlife!

 Remember to top up the water if the pond begins to dry out.

These plants keep the pond water
clean and filled with oxygen:

HORNWORT
(an underwater plant)

MARSH MARIGOLD
(grows at the edge of the pond)

☰ NATURE NOTE ☰

One of the frogs made
its home in the plant pot
I put on its side near the
edge of the pond!

Frogs are important! They
eat insects and provide
food for other animals
like birds and snakes.

I can't wait to see what
other creatures find
my pond and move in!

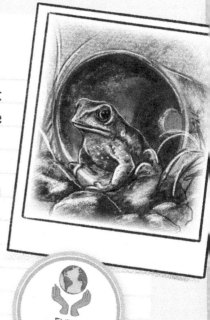

EVERY
LITTLE THING
MATTERS

bird

water boatman

hedgeho[g]

dragonfly larva

dragonfly

frogspawn

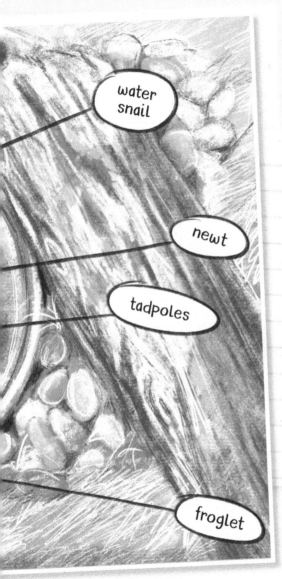

water snail

newt

tadpoles

froglet

EVERY LITTLE THING MATTERS

Samira says a little pond matters a lot!

It helps every little thing in my garden by providing it with water, food and breeding places.

⋝ MY WORMERY ⋜

I collected some worms from my garden and
made a wormery so I could watch them working.

I cut the top off
a big two-litre
plastic bottle.

Worm food (dry
leaves, some fruit
and vegetable
peelings)

Some worms
from my garden

Soil

Garden sand

Soil

Small rocks

Water spritzer:
Worms need
water every
day, but not
too wet or
they might
drown.

Worms like it dark!
I wrapped a sheet of dark
paper around my wormery.

ONE WEEK LATER

♥ The layers disappeared as the sand and soil mixed together. Channels appeared where the worms burrowed.

♥ The food from the top was dragged downwards.

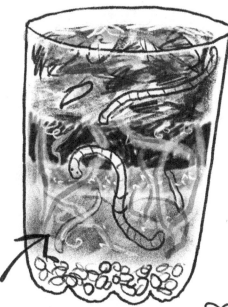

This is where the worms burrowed. They swallowed up the soil and food and pooed it out. Now the soil is great for growing things.

 NOTE: I recycled the bottle.

I put the worms back in the garden!

SAMIRA'S
CONSERVATION CORNER

Are you helping to protect nature in your garden or neighbourhood, like Lottie? Then you're a conservationist.

All over the world, conservationists are working hard to prevent species from becoming extinct.

EVERY
LITTLE THING
MATTERS

♡ WHAT YOU CAN DO: ♡

Everything in nature is connected so it's important to help save all plants and animals!

Samira

Without **ants**, for example, many species of anteaters would become extinct.
All eight species of spiny anteaters, called the pangolins, are endangered because they are hunted for their scales and meat.

Pangolin

The Lemur Leaf Frog

The **lemur leaf frog** is critically endangered because of disease and habitat changes. Conservation experts in Costa Rica started a special breeding programme, plus other zoos around the world are also working to save it.

IT'S ALWAYS WILD WITH LOTTIE ABOUT!

LOTTIE L♥VES NATURE

Bee-ware!

BY JANE CLARKE ILLUSTRATED BY JAMES BROWN

Lottie's determined to save the bugs and bees in her neighbour's garden. Can she do it before Mr Parfitt calls the exterminator?

COMING IN 2021